Granny *and* the Loch Ness Monster

3 Monster Stories:

We Go Monster Hunting

Is that the Loch Ness Monster?

But Where's the Loch Ness Monster? In the USA?

WRITTEN BY

David McNiven

ILLUSTRATED BY

Margaret Anne Suggs

ISBN 9780993168819

Also by David McNiven and Margaret Anne Suggs:
Me Nan found a Leprechaun

Granny
and
the Loch Ness Monster

We Go Monster Hunting

've a lovely Granny and Grandpa.
We all live down in Troon.
I often have my tea with them
If it's a sunny afternoon.

Troon's a Scottish seaside town
with a lovely, sandy bay
Gran says, "Your Grandpa loves it here.
He goes swimming every day."

He's teaching me the bagpipes!
He plays in the Troon Pipe Band.
Some evenings in the summer,
They play marches on the sand.

People pay a lot of money
to come and hear him play.
But my neighbors pay me money,
and say, "Please, PLEASE go away!"

WAIL

SCREECH

He said, "We're all going camping.
We'll maybe hunt big game.
We'll go hunting for that monster,
and Nessie is its name.

He laughed, "I'll need your help to pack.
I should have bought a bus -
With the tent and all the gear in here,
there's no room left for us."

"Put these boots, coats and fishing rods
in front of your seat on the floor.
Then you sit on my pipe case
so that I can close the door."

We left early the next morning
on a brilliant sunny day.
If you're ever driving to Loch Ness
it's a very long, long way.

are we there yet?

LOCH NESS

INVERNESS

glasgow

I kept asking, "Are we there yet?"
'Til he turned round a big tree,
and there it was, this huge Loch Ness
as far as you could see.

He jumped out of the car and cheered,
"That view would make you swoon!
We'll have to get the pipes out
and play Nessie a wee tune."

ut first we'll put up the folding chairs
and all that kitchen stuff.
Now help me with this massive tent,
it's surely big enough!"

"We've got tubes and bends and angles
and then there's all these clips.
Now you pull up that cover
and we'll tighten those two zips!"

And there it was; our lovely tent
in bright oranges and yellow,
and Grandpa shook my hand and laughed
"Aren't you a clever fellow?"

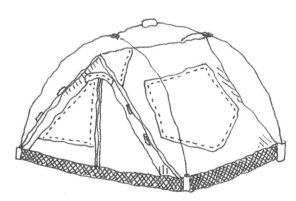

He whooped, "That water's lovely!
Hey, I think I'll have a swim."
But he didn't take his clothes off -
he just suddenly jumped in.

 yelled, "What about the monster?"
He laughed, "Don't be a dunce!
I've been swimming here for years now,
and I haven't seen him once!"

"You'll have to be my look out.
You can climb up in that tree,
and if you see him coming -
you just shout across to me."

Then I yelled, "The monster's coming!
He's out there plain to see."
He laughed, "Oh don't be silly.
It's just a floating tree!"

"Look," he said, "it's hollow.
See, I can swim straight through."
Then suddenly he yelled, "LOOK OUT!"
and disappeared from view!

Gran shouted, "Ed, stop messing!"
and "Edward, now don't tease."
Then, "Help, my Edward's missing!
Oh, someone help me, please!"

But then the log exploded -
just burst open with a crack
and there's the Loch Ness Monster
and it's swimming on its back!

But next it turned right over,
in a moment just like that -
and hanging off the monster's tail
was my poor Grandpa's hat!

I turned to look at Granny.
She shrieked, "Did you see that?
I think poor Grandpa's done for!
Look, it's got his kilt and hat!"

It clambered out of the water
and knocked down a massive tree.
I screamed to Gran "Come on, Gran, run!
It's after you and me!"

It crashed straight through the campsite!
Gran screamed in disbelief.
Its feet were big as dustbin lids
and its mouth was full of teeth!

It grabbed our lovely yellow tent
and then threw it up a tree
and a family ran in panic
as it ate their picnic tea.

We ran up to the main road,
where we stopped a passing lorry.
The man said, "Hop in quick now!
I'll help you - don't you worry."

Gran ran to tell a policeman
how her Ed went for a swim.
"Now we really don't know what to do
with that monster after him."

He asked, "Now is this a missing person?
Or is it just another hoax?
You know this Loch Ness Monster thing
confuses loads of folks!"

"Now missus, don't you worry.
Take this advice from me.
We'll just go back to your campsite
and he'll be sitting drinking tea."

He drove us to our campsite
and there to our surprise,
sat my lovely, lovely Grandpa
with a glazed look in his eyes.

He said, "The campsite's in an awful state.
It's a total mystery to me.
Just look our lovely yellow tent -
it's up there in that tree!"

"But you didn't see the Monster?"

exclaimed Gran in disbelief.
"This day's been a disaster,
but you're safe. What a relief!"

The policeman laughed, "Well, there you are!
That monster's just a hoax -
a story someone just made up
to bring the tourist folks!"

Is That the Loch Ness Monster?

today we called on Granny
and my Grandpa down at Troon.
I often go for tea and cake
on a sunny afternoon.

I told them of our school trip.
I said, "You'll never guess!
We're going to see THE MONSTER
that's up there in Loch Ness!"

Grandpa laughed, "The Loch Ness Monster?
Now, don't be such a dunce.
You know I've been there loads of times,
and haven't seen him once!"

e ate some chocolate cake and said,
"I've got the strangest feeling."
Then suddenly he yelled, "LOOK OUT!"
and grew straight through the ceiling!

He hadn't finished there now.
Please believe this tale I tell.
For we ran upstairs to find he'd gone -
straight through the roof as well!

When Grandpa's head broke through the roof
it made the whole town shake
and all the folks ran out to shout,
"It must be an EARTHQUAKE!"

But then they all just stood in awe,
because they had never seen
a dinosaur through someone's roof.
And it's such a lovely green!

"**Where** did it come from?" someone asked,
"Did it fall out of the sky?"
"Oh, surely not," a teacher said.
"Those dinosaurs can't fly."

 schoolboy asked, "What do they eat?
And do they TEAR and CHEW?"
A policeman yelled, "Hey you! Keep back -
his next meal could be you!"

My Gran came running out and yelled,
"Just look up there by jiminey!
It's eaten half a dozen slates,
and started on the chimney!"

The fire brigade came on the scene
with their siren and a bell.
And someone said, "Best call the zoo."
So some keepers came as well!

Gran shrieked, "It's my poor Edward,
and something must be done!"
A priest arrived, he said a prayer,
and so did a nice nun.

"Hey, that's Nessius Neversaurus!"
shouted old Professor Moore,
"Yes, that's the Loch Ness Monster,
I am absolutely sure."

The media men were next to come,
with the TV and the press.
So Granny said, "I'll slip upstairs
and put on my new dress."

Special soldiers came from nowhere -
no one knew who they were.
The one in charge was very posh.
The others called him 'Sir'.

Next the Ministry of Ag arrived
in white protective suits,
with drums of disinfectant
and big, green welly boots.

"**We're** to be *what*?" shrieked my Granny.
I could tell she was annoyed,
"All sprayed with disinfectant?
My new dress will be destroyed!"

A fireman said, "We'll get him out.
Just pull down that end wall."
A soldier laughed, "Oh, don't be daft!
He's fifteen feet too tall!"

They sent for a huge yellow crane,
and worked late into the night,
but Grandpa didn't move an inch -
Poor soul was stuck so tight.

I wakened the next morning,
our Loch Ness Monster had gone.
Grandpa was in the kitchen
and all his clothes were torn.

He said, "We're in an awful state,
and half our roof has gone.
I can't remember anything -
Were we hit by a bomb?"

"A bomb?" yelled out my Granny,
"You just haven't got a clue!
This wasn't done by any bomb!
This mess was made by YOU!"

"By ME?" chuckled my Grandpa,
"Was I in some sort of rage . . . ?
Hey, they've found the Loch Ness Monster.
Look, here on the front page!"

As Grandpa turned the pages
he gasped, "Oh, what a mess!"
The last time that I felt like this
I'd been swimming in Loch Ness!"

Gran said, "Oh, I remember well.
You were missing half the day.
When we got back to the campsite,
you didn't know you'd been away."

"I was sure that you'd been eaten.
We were all in such distress,
because that day **we saw the monster**
out there swimming in Loch Ness!"

"But I never saw the monster,"
gasped Grandpa. "Don't you see?
There wasn't any monster -

the Loch Ness
Monster's... ME !"

So now you've read my story.
My question is, I guess,
Will we see the Loch Ness Monster
on our bus trip to Loch Ness?

But Where's the Loch Ness Monster? In the USA?

Grandpa is the Loch Ness Monster.
It sounds crazy but it's true,
and how or why he does it
he just hasn't got a clue.

He found out for the first time
there with Granny home at Troon.
We'd gone to her for tea and cake
one Sunday afternoon.

We were sitting eating cake. He said,
"I've got the strangest feeling."
Then suddenly he yelled, "LOOK OUT!"
And grew STRAIGHT THROUGH the ceiling!

He crashed and broke straight through the roof
until his head poked out.
And all the folks came out to ask,
"How will you get him out?"

Then a helicopter landed,
a big man with loads of cash.
He strolled across, cigar in hand,
then stopped to flick some ash.

He said, "I'll pay five million dollars,
I don't care what it takes.
The folks back home will love him.
We'll take him to The States."

ran laughed, "It's my poor Edward!
I don't care what you pay.
He doesn't like to travel far . . .
. . . Eh, how much did you say?"

So, we're all millionaires now!
We're sailing to New York.
We were going to fly by jumbo jet
but they said it wouldn't work.

The pilot came to talk to us.
He said, "You cannot fly.
If you turn into that monster thing
we'll fall out of the sky!"

We're in a brilliant cabin,
on this ship like a hotel.
There's lots of fancy food to eat
and nightly shows as well.

The band play brilliant music,
and we all eat around the pool.
A magician does amazing tricks
and a clown just acts the fool.

grandpa laughed, "That water's lovely.
I'll have to take a swim."
But he didn't take his clothes off.
He just suddenly jumped in!

The passengers were laughing-
the clown caused such a scene.
Then suddenly Grandpa yelled,

and grew and turned *that* green!

 man yelled, "That's real magic.
Gee, say how did he do that?"
Then the monster swung his tail around
and hit the poor man - SPLAT!

He knocked over the chef's buffet
then ate the meringue swan,
and they couldn't stop him eating
until the chocolate cake had gone.

Some people started laughing,
while others screamed in fright.
Then he climbed onto the afterdeck
and jumped off into the night.

The Captain yelled, "Stop engines!
Quick, turn on all the lights!
Be careful how you catch it lads -
I don't know if it bites!"

hey launched some little rescue boats
which circled round and round
to search for man or monster -
but neither could be found.

The captain sent an S.O.S.
to warn all ships and craft.
Gran sobbed, "They'll never find him.
The whole idea's just daft."

But the Captain came next morning.
He laughed, "You'll never guess.
A fishing boat has found a man
in the sea near Inverness!"

When we docked later in New York
there was TV and the press.
Gran said, "I'm sorry gentlemen,
my Ed's gone to Inverness!"

The helicopter man arrived,
he said, "Hey folks, where's Ed?"
Gran said, "I'm really sorry sir,
he's in Inverness instead."

new
york
USA

Gran sobbed, "Truly, I am sorry.
It's a mystery to me.
He just became the Loch Ness Monster,
and jumped into the sea."

He yelled, "You cannot do this!
I've got the whole thing planned.
My Loch Ness Park is finished!
I've booked the Inverness pipe band!"

His face went red and redder still.
He shrieked, "You've gone too far.
Our President's to cut the tape.
He gave me this cigar!"

"I've got monster rides and monster caves,
monster everything, I guess.
But where's the Loch Ness Monster . . . ?
Say, that sounds just like Loch Ness!"

he smiled for just a moment
and laughed, "That's it, oh yes!
It's just like those Scottish stories:
WHERE'S THE MONSTER IN LOCH NESS?"

"I guess we'll go ahead without him.
Say, we'll carry on as planned.
We may not have a monster,
but we've the INVERNESS PIPE BAND!"

ext day we were guests of honour
at the opening, oh so grand,
and marching past the President
were the INVERNESS PIPE BAND!!

Gran said, "That band just isn't right.
It's really got me thinking.
Watch: every time the band march past -
that PIPER THERE - he's winking!"

When the band had finished playing,
we ran outside to see.
Then my lovely Grandpa waved to us
and called "Cooeee, it's me!"

"Now you're wondering how I got here?
No it wasn't as we planned.
I just dressed up as a piper,
then I flew here with the band."

"**This** Loch Ness Park is quite a place!
Och, I'll have to have a swim!"
But he kept his kilt and sporran on,
then ran and dived straight in.

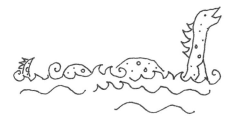

Well, he caused such a commotion
and the band made such a scene,
then suddenly he yelled, "LOOK OUT!"
and turned that lovely green.

He grew and grew up to the sky
then swam out in 'Loch Ness'.
Well, the helicopter man went mad
and screamed, "Oh yes, oh yes!"

all the people started cheering,
and the gates were opened wide,
and they all ate monster burgers
and rode those monster rides.

The press took lots of photos,
and I shook the President's hand.
He said, "Gee, your Grandpa's quite a guy.
Was he playing in the band?"

but if the monster's out there swimming
the puzzle is, I guess,
could there be another monster
back in Scotland in Loch Ness?